DRUG ADDICTION AND RECOVERY

Hallucinogens:
Ecstasy, LSD, and Ketamine

DRUG ADDICTION AND RECOVERY

Alcohol and Tobacco

Causes of Drug Use

Drug Use and Mental Health

Drug Use and the Family

Drug Use and the Law

Hallucinogens: Ecstasy, LSD, and Ketamine

Intervention and Recovery

Marijuana and Synthetics

Opioids: Heroin, OxyContin, and Painkillers

Over-the-Counter Drugs

Performance-Enhancing Drugs: Steroids, Hormones, and Supplements

Prescription Drugs

Stimulants: Meth, Cocaine, and Amphetamines

DRUG ADDICTION AND RECOVERY

Hallucinogens:
Ecstasy, LSD, and Ketamine

John Perritano

SERIES CONSULTANT
SARA BECKER, Ph.D.
Brown University School of Public Health
Warren Alpert Medical School

MASON CREST

Mason Crest
450 Parkway Drive, Suite D
Broomall, PA 19008
www.masoncrest.com

© 2017 by Mason Crest, an imprint of National Highlights, Inc. All rights reserved.
No part of this publication may be reproduced or transmitted in any form or by any means, electronic or mechanical, including photocopying, recording, taping, or any information storage and retrieval system, without permission from the publisher.

MTM Publishing, Inc.
www.mtmpublishing.com

President: Valerie Tomaselli
Vice President, Book Development: Hilary Poole
Designer: Annemarie Redmond
Copyeditor: Peter Jaskowiak
Editorial Assistant: Andrea St. Aubin

Series ISBN: 978-1-4222-3598-0
Hardback ISBN: 978-1-4222-3604-8
E-Book ISBN: 978-1-4222-8248-9

Cataloging-in-Publication Data on file with the Library of Congress

Printed and bound in the United States of America.

First printing
9 8 7 6 5 4 3 2 1

QR CODES AND LINKS TO THIRD PARTY CONTENT
You may gain access to certain third party content ("Third Party Sites") by scanning and using the QR Codes that appear in this publication (the "QR Codes"). We do not operate or control in any respect any information, products or services on such Third Party Sites linked to by us via the QR Codes included in this publication and we assume no responsibility for any materials you may access using the QR Codes. Your use of the QR Codes may be subject to terms, limitations, or restrictions set forth in the applicable terms of use or otherwise established by the owners of the Third Party Sites. Our linking to such Third Party Sites via the QR Codes does not imply an endorsement or sponsorship of such Third Party Sites, or the information, products or services offered on or through the Third Party Sites, nor does it imply an endorsement or sponsorship of this publication by the owners of such Third Party Sites.

TABLE OF CONTENTS

Series Introduction 6
Chapter One: What Are Hallucinogens? 11
Chapter Two: LSD and Other Classic Hallucinogens 21
Chapter Three: Ecstasy (MDMA) 35
Chapter Four: Dissociative Drugs 45
Further Reading 58
Educational Videos 59
Series Glossary 60
Index 61
About the Author 64
About the Advisor 64
Photo Credits 64

Key Icons to Look for:

Words to Understand: These words with their easy-to-understand definitions will increase the reader's understanding of the text, while building vocabulary skills.

Sidebars: This boxed material within the main text allows readers to build knowledge, gain insights, explore possibilities, and broaden their perspectives by weaving together additional information to provide realistic and holistic perspectives.

Research Projects: Readers are pointed toward areas of further inquiry connected to each chapter. Suggestions are provided for projects that encourage deeper research and analysis.

Text-Dependent Questions: These questions send the reader back to the text for more careful attention to the evidence presented there.

Educational Videos: Readers can view videos by scanning our QR codes, providing them with additional educational content to supplement the text. Examples include news coverage, moments in history, speeches, iconic sports moments and much more!

Series Glossary of Key Terms: This back-of-the-book glossary contains terminology used throughout the series. Words found here increase the reader's ability to read and comprehend higher-level books and articles in this field.

SERIES INTRODUCTION

Many adolescents in the United States will experiment with alcohol or other drugs by time they finish high school. According to a 2014 study funded by the National Institute on Drug Abuse, about 27 percent of 8th graders have tried alcohol, 20 percent have tried drugs, and 13 percent have tried cigarettes. By 12th grade, these rates more than double: 66 percent of 12th graders have tried alcohol, 50 percent have tried drugs, and 35 percent have tried cigarettes.

Adolescents who use substances experience an increased risk of a wide range of negative consequences, including physical injury, family conflict, school truancy, legal problems, and sexually transmitted diseases. Higher rates of substance use are also associated with the leading causes of death in this age group: accidents, suicide, and violent crime. Relative to adults, adolescents who experiment with alcohol or other drugs progress more quickly to a full-blown substance use disorder and have more co-occurring mental health problems.

The National Survey on Drug Use and Health (NSDUH) estimated that in 2015 about 1.3 million adolescents between the ages of 12 and 17 (5 percent of adolescents in the United States) met the medical criteria for a substance use disorder. Unfortunately, the vast majority of these

> **IF YOU NEED HELP NOW . . .**
>
> **SAMHSA's National Helpline provides referrals for mental-health or substance-use counseling.**
> 1-800-662-HELP (4357) or https://findtreatment.samhsa.gov
>
> **SAMHSA's National Suicide Prevention Lifeline provides crisis counseling by phone or online, 24-hours-a-day and 7 days a week.**
> 1-800-273-TALK (8255) or http://www.suicidepreventionlifeline.org

When pro- and anti-drug information sit side-by-side online, it can be hard for kids to separate fact from fiction.

adolescents did not receive treatment. Less than 10 percent of those with a diagnosis received specialty care, leaving 1.2 million adolescents with an unmet need for treatment.

The NSDUH asked the 1.2 million adolescents with untreated substance use disorders why they didn't receive specialty care. Over 95 percent said that they didn't think they needed it. The other 5 percent reported challenges finding quality treatment that was covered by their insurance. Very few treatment providers and agencies offer substance use treatment designed to meet the specific needs of adolescents. Meanwhile, numerous insurance plans have "opted out" of providing coverage for addiction treatment, while others have placed restrictions on what is covered.

Stigma about substance use is another serious problem. We don't call a person with an eating disorder a "food abuser," but we use terms like "drug abuser" to describe individuals with substance use disorders. Even treatment providers often unintentionally use judgmental words, such as describing urine screen results as either "clean" or "dirty." Underlying this language is the idea that a substance use disorder is some kind of moral failing or character flaw, and that people with these disorders deserve blame or punishment for their struggles.

And punish we do. A 2010 report by CASA Columbia found that in the United States, 65 percent of the 2.3 million people in prisons and jails met medical criteria for a substance use disorder, while another 20 percent had histories of substance use disorders, committed their crimes while under the influence of alcohol or drugs, or committed a substance-related crime. Many of these inmates spend decades in prison, but only 11 percent of them receive any treatment during their incarceration. Our society invests significantly more money in punishing individuals with substance use disorders than we do in treating them.

At a basic level, the ways our society approaches drugs and alcohol—declaring a "war on drugs," for example, or telling kids to "Just Say No!"—reflect a misunderstanding about the nature of addiction. The reality is that addiction is a disease that affects all types of people—parents and children, rich and poor, young and old. Substance use disorders stem from a complex interplay of genes, biology, and the environment, much like most physical and mental illnesses.

The way we talk about recovery, using phrases like "kick the habit" or "breaking free," also misses the mark. Substance use disorders are chronic, insidious, and debilitating illnesses. Fortunately, there are a number of effective treatments for substance use disorders. For many patients, however, the road is long and hard. Individuals recovering from substance use disorders can experience horrible withdrawal symptoms, and many will continue to struggle with cravings for alcohol or drugs. It can be a daily struggle to cope with these cravings and stay abstinent. A popular saying at Alcoholics Anonymous (AA) meetings is "one day at a time," because every day of recovery should be respected and celebrated.

There are a lot of incorrect stereotypes about individuals with substance use disorders, and there is a lot of false information about the substances, too. If you do an Internet search on the term "marijuana," for instance, two top hits are a web page by the National Institute on Drug Abuse and a page operated by Weedmaps, a medical and recreational marijuana dispensary. One of these pages publishes scientific information and one publishes pro-marijuana articles. Both pages have a high-quality, professional appearance. If you had never heard of either organization, it would be hard to know which to trust. It can be really difficult for the average person, much less the average teenager, to navigate these waters.

The topics covered in this series were specifically selected to be relevant to teenagers. About half of the volumes cover the types of drugs that they are most likely to hear about or to come in contact with. The other half cover important issues related to alcohol and other drug use (which we refer to as "drug use" in the titles for simplicity). These books cover topics such as the causes of drug use, the influence of drug use on the family, drug use and the legal system, drug use and mental health, and treatment options. Many teens will either have personal experience with these issues or will know someone who does.

This series was written to help young people get the facts about common drugs, substance use disorders, substance-related problems, and recovery. Accurate information can help adolescents to make better decisions. Students who are educated can help each other to better understand the risks and consequences of drug use. Facts also go a long way to reducing the stigma associated with substance use. We tend to fear or avoid things that we don't understand. Knowing the facts can make it easier to support each other. For students who know someone struggling with a substance use disorder, these books can also help them know what to expect. If they are worried about someone, or even about themselves, these books can help to provide some answers and a place to start.

—Sara J. Becker, Ph.D., Assistant Professor (Research), Center for Alcohol and Addictions Studies, Brown University School of Public Health, Assistant Professor (Research), Department of Psychiatry and Human Behavior, Brown University Medical School

WORDS TO UNDERSTAND

alkaloids: nitrogen-based compounds found in plants that can effect a person's nervous system.

entheogenic: ability to bring on a religious experience.

hallucinate: seeing things that aren't there; something that makes a person hallucinate is called a hallucinogenic.

neurotransmitter: a chemical that carries messages between nerve cells.

psychedelic: a term that describes the effect of hallucinogenic drugs.

psychotropic: capable of affecting the mind.

CHAPTER ONE

WHAT ARE HALLUCINOGENS?

At the turn of the 20th century, archaeologists discovered the ancient "mushroom stones" of Guatemala. Carved by hand around 1000 BCE, they show individuals with strange, umbrella-like canopies on tops of their heads. These strange stones were found not only in Guatemala, but all across Mesoamerica, a region that now covers central Mexico, Belize, Guatemala, El Salvador, Honduras, Nicaragua, and northern Costa Rica. At first, many assumed the stones were somehow associated with male fertility.

Some scientists, however, disagreed. In their opinion, these stones represented "magic mushrooms" that cause people to hallucinate when consumed. Inside the mushrooms was a chemical compound called psilocybin that caused people to see things that weren't there. The ancient Americans worshipped the mushrooms as gods and the intricately carved stones were symbols of that belief. Scientists suspected mushroom cults that flourished in the Americas long before Europeans arrived in 1492 used the mushroom stones as part of an ancient religious ceremony. Those in the cults ingested the hallucinogenic mushrooms, creating an **entheogenic** effect, the ability to bring on a spiritual experience. Every Mesoamerican civilization that flourished 2,000 to 3,000 years ago, including the Olmecs, the Mayas, and the Aztecs, used magic mushrooms in religious rituals. These civilizations also used other hallucinogenic herbs, plants, and animals to alter their state of mind and to treat illnesses.

Franciso Javier Carod-Artal, an expert on the subject, says early American civilizations used **psychedelic** honey, toads, and toloache, the "devil's herb," which they brewed into tea to communicate with their gods and ancestors. People who were to be sacrificed to the gods drank the beverage before execution. "It has been hypothesized that during ritual human sacrifices, some prisoners and those people that would be sacrificed were drunk with some conscious-altering beverages, probably ones including toloache," Carod-Artal writes.

An Olmec altar in Tabasco, Mexico. The Olmecs used hallucinogens as part of their religious worship.

CHAPTER ONE: WHAT ARE HALLUCINOGENS?

FLESH OF THE GODS

The Aztecs called the magic mushrooms *teonanácatl*, or "flesh of the gods." Spanish conquistadors, all of whom were Christian, called the mushrooms "flesh of the devil." They tried to stamp out the use of the mushrooms by torturing and murdering the Aztecs. Modern-day scientists believe that at least 54 hallucinogenic mushrooms grew in the Mesoamerica long before the Spanish arrived.

ALTERNATE STATES OF BEING

Magic mushrooms and other hallucinogenic substances are still used today by those seeking some sort of mystical religious experience or, at the very least, a different state of consciousness. Hallucinogens, such as LSD, can be made in a laboratory by humans, while others, such as salvia, are found in plants or their extracts.

There are several categories of hallucinogenic drugs. One is *psychedelics*. LSD is an example of a psychedelic drug, as are magic mushrooms. Another common psychedelic is called mescaline. Psychedelics distort time and reality. They can lead a user to believe that he or she is undergoing a spiritual experience. Ecstasy, which is the most popular hallucinogen, has properties similar to the psychedelic mescaline and the stimulant amphetamine.

Dissociative drugs, including PCP, also known as Angel Dust, and ketamine, make up another category of hallucinogens. Dissociative drugs make a person feel detached from reality. People taking dissociative drugs might feel as if they are having "out-of-body" experiences. Dissociative drugs produce hallucinations, dreamlike visions, and a euphoric high.

14 HALLUCINOGENS: ECSTASY, LSD, AND KETAMINE

An example of LSD blotter paper, in a photo taken by the Drug Enforcement Agency. The ruler is in centimeters, showing how tiny each dose actually is.

According to the most recent statistics compiled by the federal government's Substance Abuse and Mental Health Services Administration (SAMHSA), nearly 1 million people aged 12 or older used a hallucinogen for the first time in 2014. During that same period, for that same age group, 287,000 used LSD for the first time, and 609,000 used Ecstasy.

HOW DO HALLUCINOGENS WORK?

Although the exact nature of how hallucinogens affect the brain is not known, most hallucinogens contain nitrogen and are classified as alkaloids. Alkaloids are often found in poisons. Many hallucinogenic drugs mimic several neurotransmitters that the body creates naturally, including serotonin, acetylcholine, or catecholamine. Neurotransmitters are chemicals that allow brain cells, or neurons, to communicate with each other. Serotonin is a chemical that scientists believe regulates a person's mood. Acetylcholine plays a role in muscle movement, while catecholamine is released into the blood when a person is under physical or emotional stress.

Most researchers suspect the drugs work, in part, by interfering with the actions of neurotransmitters as they bind with their receptor sites on cells. The receptors show up in various places in the brain, including the thalamus, which is responsible for relaying messages to the cortex, the part of the brain that's responsible for sensory perception.

EFFECTS OF HALLUCINOGENS

Hallucinogens powerfully alter a perception's sense of reality by distorting the functions of a person's senses, as well as their sense of time and space. A person who take a hallucinogenic "trip" will often report a "seeing" sounds and "hearing" colors. It's a phenomenon called *synesthesia*—the production of an impression from one sense (for example, sight) by the stimulation of another sense (for example, hearing). In people who don't use hallucinogens, synesthesia is a real and rare neurological disorder, although its causes are a mystery.

Some people who use hallucinogen drugs experience a rare but frightening condition known as hallucinogen persisting perception disorder (HPPD). HPPD occurs when a person undergoes persistent, long-term hallucinations that continue after the drug should have worn off. People suffering from HPPD might see something move in their peripheral field of vision that isn't there. They might see blurred patterns or flashes of different colors. Such hallucinations might last seconds or minutes. HPPD can last for months, years, or for the rest of a person's life. A person does not have to misuse a drug to any great extent for HPPD to set in. There have been reports of some people having a sudden onset of HPPD after just one use of hallucinogens.

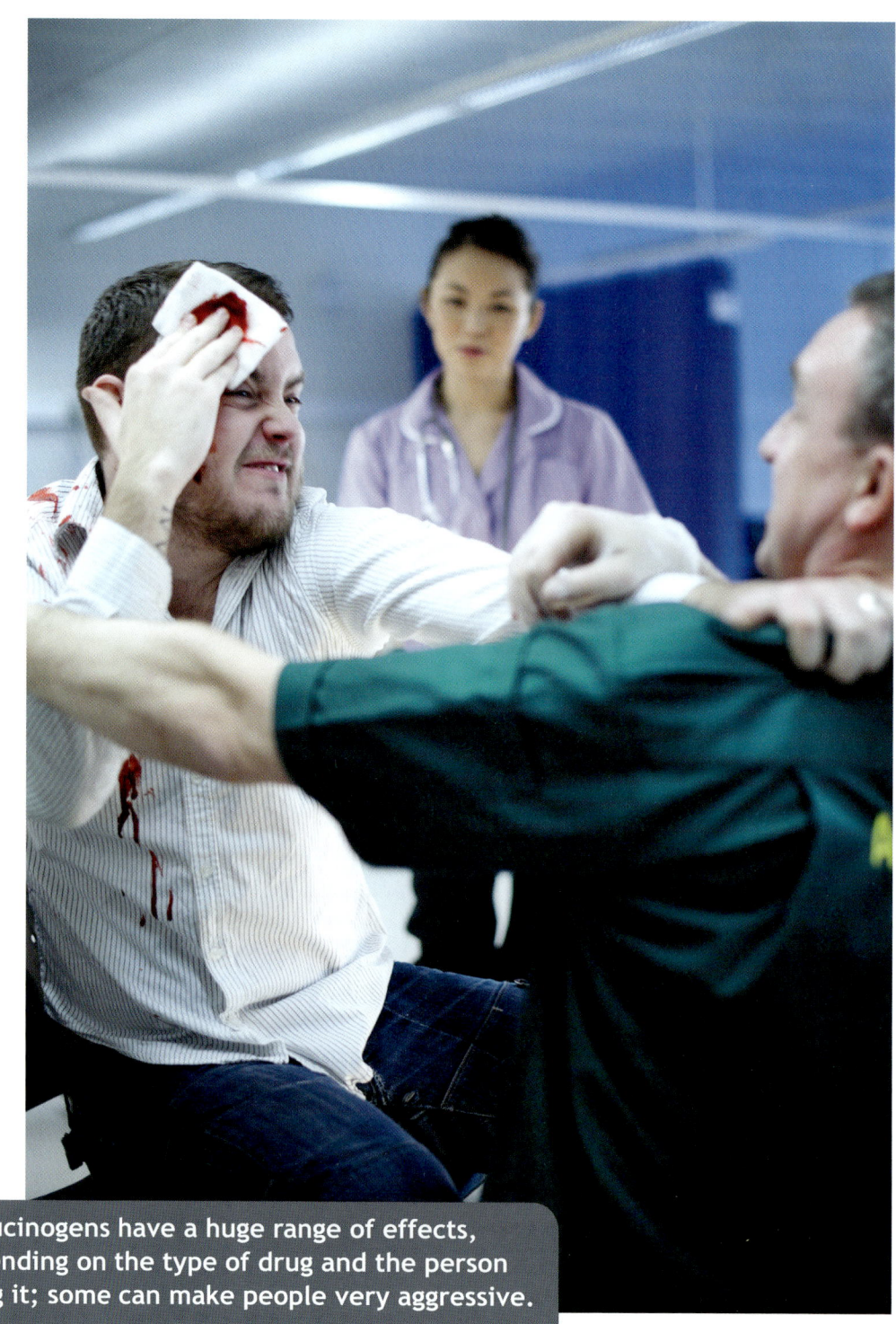

Hallucinogens have a huge range of effects, depending on the type of drug and the person using it; some can make people very aggressive.

HOW MANY PEOPLE HAVE HPPD?

Doctors have known about HPPD for years, but it is hard to figure out how many people it affects. In 2010, scientists conducted an online survey questioning over 2,500 users of hallucinogens. They found that about 1 out of 25 wanted to seek treatment for visual symptoms they believe were HPPD related. Some researchers have argued that this estimate is low, because the study did not represent those who rarely used hallucinogens, and only a small portion of those surveyed had actively sought medical care.

Other researchers, however, have argued that this estimate is high, because people with HPPD-symptoms may have been more likely to take the time to complete the survey, creating skewed results. In a review of the literature by Harvard Medical School researchers, the authors concluded that "the data do not permit us to estimate, even crudely, the prevalence of 'strict' HPPD." Still, the number of monthly visitors (9,000) on the website HPPDonline.com suggests that the issue is very real for many people.

A person with HPPD knows that the hallucinations are not real, but that doesn't mean they aren't startling. Scientists studying the condition say that 65 percent of HPPD patients suffer from panic attacks, while 50 percent suffer from major depression. Many say they experience numbness, tingling, throbbing, and burning sensations. "I have had full blown hallucinations a few times without drugs," one user wrote.

TREATMENT FOR HALLUCINOGENS

Hallucinogens are not like most categories of drugs. Some, such as PCP, have addictive qualities, while others, such as LSD, do not. Unlike other drugs, such as heroin, the focus of hallucinogenic treatment is not necessarily long term. Particularly for LSD and other psychedelics, treatment often focuses on short-term crisis management, especially if a person is on a "bad trip." A person might have to be sedated for a time if he or she exhibits hostile or aggressive behavior.

Inpatient or outpatient therapy is recommend when hallucinogenic use has led to acute or impairing psychotic symptoms, especially when it occurs alongside a serious mood disorder, other substance abuse problems, or eating disorders. Such programs include support-group therapy and cognitive-behavioral therapy (CBT), in which a person learns how to deal effectively with situations that she or he cannot control.

MEDICAL MUSHROOMS

In recent years, doctors have begun to understand that the main ingredient in magical mushrooms might have medicinal purposes, something ancient Americans understood well. Doctors have begun to give psychotropic mushrooms to their patients to help ease the anxiety that accompanies late-stage cancers, for example, while others are studying whether psilocybin can be used to treat people with depression. Psilocybin reboots the brain and establishes new neural pathways, or connections, between parts of the brain that play a role in consciousness.

Scientists have also conducted studies on whether psilocybin can be used to treat those suffering from post-traumatic stress disorder, a mental condition that results from a traumatic event. Studies on mice show that the substance wipes out bad memories and spurs new brain cell growth. But studying psilocybin in the United States is problematic because the drug is illegal.

CHAPTER ONE: WHAT ARE HALLUCINOGENS?

Although full-blown hallucinogen addiction is very rare, heavy users may find that support groups can help them learn skills to avoid needing the drug so often.

TEXT-DEPENDENT QUESTIONS

1. What is the main mind-bending ingredient in magic mushrooms?
2. What are the three main types of hallucinogens?
3. What is synesthesia?

RESEARCH PROJECT

Create a map of the Americas and use different colors to shade in the territory where each of these civilizations lived: Olmec, Aztec, and Maya. Create a key for your map that includes the dates each civilization flourished.

WORDS TO UNDERSTAND

counterculture: ways of behaving that are deliberately different from the normal culture values of a larger society.

derivative: something that comes from, or is based on, something else.

inhibitions: feelings that restrict or hold someone back.

mescaline: an hallucinogenic alkaloid.

metabolize: the ability of a living organism to chemically change compounds.

parasitic: an organism that lives off a host, often at the host's expense.

proselytizing: attempting to convert a person to another way of thinking.

stimulant: a drug that temporarily induces improvements in either mental or physical functions.

synthesize: to produce a substance using a chemical process.

CHAPTER TWO

LSD AND OTHER CLASSIC HALLUCINOGENS

Lysergic acid diethylamide (LSD) is one of the best-known hallucinogenic drugs. According to the National Institute on Drug Abuse (NIDA), 1.1 percent of 8th graders, 2.6 percent of 10th graders and 3.7 percent of 12th graders have tried LSD at least once. LSD has about 80 street names, including acid, doses, hits, yellow submarine, boomers, window pane, sugar cubes, tabs, and trips. Most doses of LSD are poured on to small squares of paper with designs on them, which are ingested by the user.

   LSD is powerful because it distorts users' sense of reality. They might see images that don't exist and hear sounds when everything is quiet. They might feel things even when they are not being touched. Such hallucinations can be pleasurable for some, and even intellectually stimulating.

22 HALLUCINOGENS: ECSTASY, LSD, AND KETAMINE

LSD is sold in a variety of forms; these pills and powder were seized by the Drug Enforcement Agency.

On the other hand, a person using LSD can have a negative, even scary, experience, or "bad trip." No two "trips" on LSD are the same. A user's experience is shaped by a variety of things, including where they are taking the drug and how long they have been using it.

A LONG STRANGE TRIP

LSD was first synthesized in a Swiss laboratory in 1938. At the time, a chemist named Albert Hofmann was working for the Sandoz Pharmaceutical Company in Basel, Switzerland. He was experimenting with a parasitic fungus called ergot, which grew on rye. Thousands of people in the Middle Ages died when eating rye bread infected by the fungus.

By the time Hofmann was conducting his experiments, scientists had already isolated the nucleus common to all ergot alkaloids and named it lysergic acid. Armed with this knowledge, Hofmann developed several derivatives of lysergic acid that he hoped would lower blood pressure and improve brain function in the elderly. Hofmann developed one derivative that he named LSD-25, which he hoped would make it easier for people to breathe, and easier for blood to circulate.

But LSD-25 did not work as Hofmann had hoped, and he abandoned his experiments. Hofmann looked again at LSD-25 five years later. As he cooked up another batch for testing, Hofmann started to feel restless and dizzy. "I lay down and sank into a not unpleasant, intoxicated-like condition characterized by an extremely stimulated imagination," he later wrote. "In a dreamlike state, with eyes closed (I found the daylight to be unpleasantly glaring), I perceived an uninterrupted stream of fantastic pictures, extraordinary shapes with intense, kaleidoscopic play of colors. After some two hours this condition faded away."

Hofmann returned to the laboratory later and intentionally took the drug. He took 10 times more than a person would take today. Historians like to say it was the world's first "acid trip." Hofmann could not speak and became delirious. He panicked and told his lab assistant to call a doctor. The doctor rushed over to the laboratory and found nothing wrong. Hofmann's panic soon gave way to euphoria. He again saw beautiful shapes and colors. He said he felt like "a demon had invaded me, had taken possession of my body, mind and soul." The next day everything was back to normal. "The world was as if newly created." He published the results of his discovery in 1943.

THE LSD COUNTERCULTURE

Sandoz Pharmaceutical Company, where Hofmann worked, saw no medical purpose for LSD, yet it provided free samples to researchers to encourage new experiments. By the 1960s, hundreds of scientific papers on the drug made the rounds of the psychiatric community. Psychiatrists began giving LSD to their patients for a variety of reasons, including helping alcoholics stay sober. One psychologist, Timothy Leary, liked the effects of the drug so much that he encouraged young people to take LSD to "turn on, tune in, and drop out."

LSD helped spawn a counterculture in the United States and elsewhere during the 1960s. By the middle of the decade, however, LSD had become a serious public health issue, as many people who had taken the drugs went on "bad trips," sometimes with dire consequences. In 1969, the daughter of TV personality Art Linkletter plunged to her death from the window of her sixth-floor Hollywood apartment under the influence of LSD.

Still, LSD overdoses that result in death are rare. Though there have been reports of LSD users experiencing heart attacks and strokes, no direct link with LSD could be firmly established. In 1973, eight people snorted a massive dose of LSD at a party thinking it was cocaine, a stimulant. Although most of them became unconscious, they eventually recovered from the accidental overdose.

The famous bus of writer Ken Kesey and his "Merry Pranksters" of the mid 1960s. LSD became strongly associated with the counterculture of that era.

LSD AND THE COLD WAR

During the 1950s and 1960s, LSD caught the attention of the military and the spy services of several nations, including the United States and the Soviet Union. Both countries experimented with LSD as a potential chemical weapon. Long before Timothy Leary was **proselytizing** about LSD, the CIA was secretly testing its effects on hundreds of unsuspecting civilians. During the 1950s and 1960s, the CIA secretly funded research experiments at over 80 institutions, including colleges and universities, hospitals, and prisons. In many cases, the experiments consisted of administering LSD to vulnerable people such as mental patients, prisoners, drug addicts, and prostitutes. The CIA then followed and observed these people to see what happened. The project was named MK-ULTRA. Under this project, LSD was given to people without their knowledge or consent, which was a clear violation of the Nuremberg Code that the United States agreed to follow after World War II.

The agency also used the drug to question spy suspects. The CIA reportedly conducted the tests because the agency was afraid the Soviets, North Koreans, and Chinese were using the drug to brainwash Americans. The CIA program was sanctioned in 1953, scaled back in 1964, and officially halted in 1973.

A person can lose all **inhibitions** and self control on LSD. In those cases, people can kill themselves in various accidental ways, such as by walking in front of a car, or, as Art Linkletter's daughter did, falling through a window. "It wasn't suicide," Linkletter said at the time, "because she wasn't herself. It was murder. She was murdered by the people who manufacture and sell LSD."

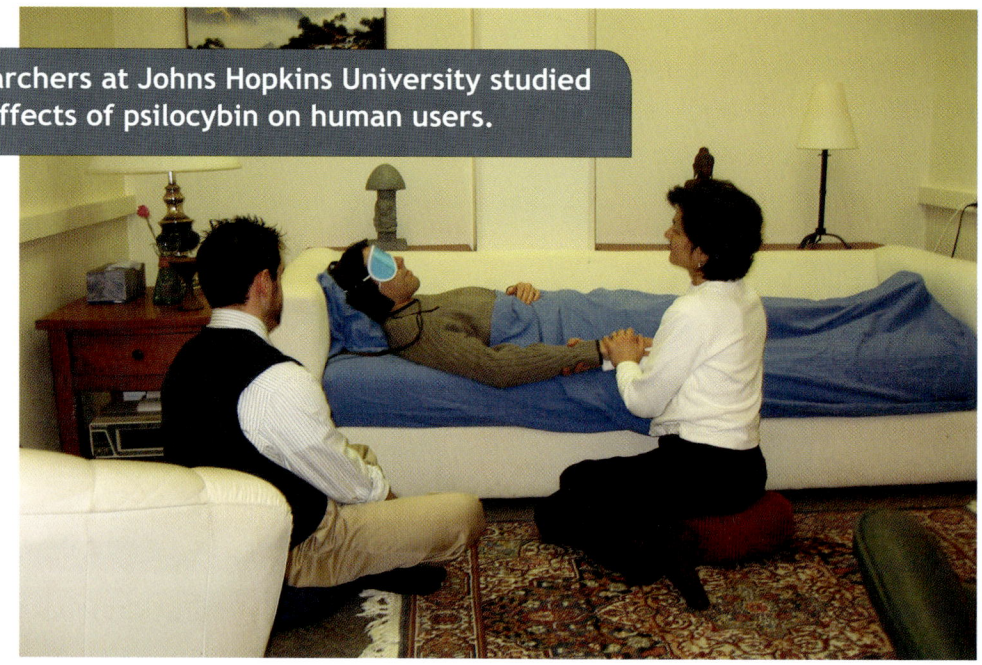

Researchers at Johns Hopkins University studied the effects of psilocybin on human users.

PHYSICAL AND MENTAL EFFECTS

Taking LSD is like rolling dice: the results are unpredictable. Matt Harvey, a reporter, took LSD when he was a freshman at Saint Bonaventure University in Alleghany, New York. He had taken the drug once before and all went fine. The second time, however, Harvey had a bad trip. He was in his dorm room after taking the drug and started smoking marijuana. Suddenly, the "room turned flat and black," he said. "Intense color wheels sparked around me. My arms and legs felt as if they were stretching into infinity."

Bad things started to happen to Harvey. He could feel his heart pounding against his chest. His roommate was afraid. His hallucinations became scarier. "Everything around me changed colors and started melting like lava. I was convinced I might lose my mind for good." Harvey didn't lose his mind, but his story illustrates the power of LSD. Chronic LSD use can create a number of problems, including depression, mania, and

CHAPTER TWO: LSD AND OTHER CLASSIC HALLUCINOGENS

schizophrenia—a serious mental disorder that affects how a person thinks, acts, and feels. Chronic LSD use can also cause flashback hallucinations, which can be unpredictable and frightening.

During an LSD trip, a person's mood can change on a dime. One moment they might feel blissful, the next moment they could be caught up in pangs of terror.

ADDICTIVE PROPERTIES

LSD is not considered a highly addictive drug. Although its effect on the brain is huge, a person does not become physically dependent on it. People don't crave LSD as they would crave heroin, alcohol, or cocaine. If a person stops taking the drug, he or she will not go through physical withdrawal.

However, a person's body can develop a tolerance to the drug, which means that after a while a regular user will need larger amounts to get

SIDE EFFECTS

Short-term effects of LSD include dizziness, insomnia, loss of appetite, and increased heart rate and body temperature. A person can also suffer from tremors, weakness, and numbness. A person can vomit or feel nauseous.

On the website of the Foundation for a Drug-Free World, a 21-year-old woman named Donna admits that taking LSD was like "eating candy," but "one night during one of my binges I blacked out and awoke with blood all over my face and vomit coming out of my mouth. By some miracle, I pulled myself awake and cleaned myself up. I got into the car, shaking, drove to my parent's house. I climbed into bed with my mom and cried."

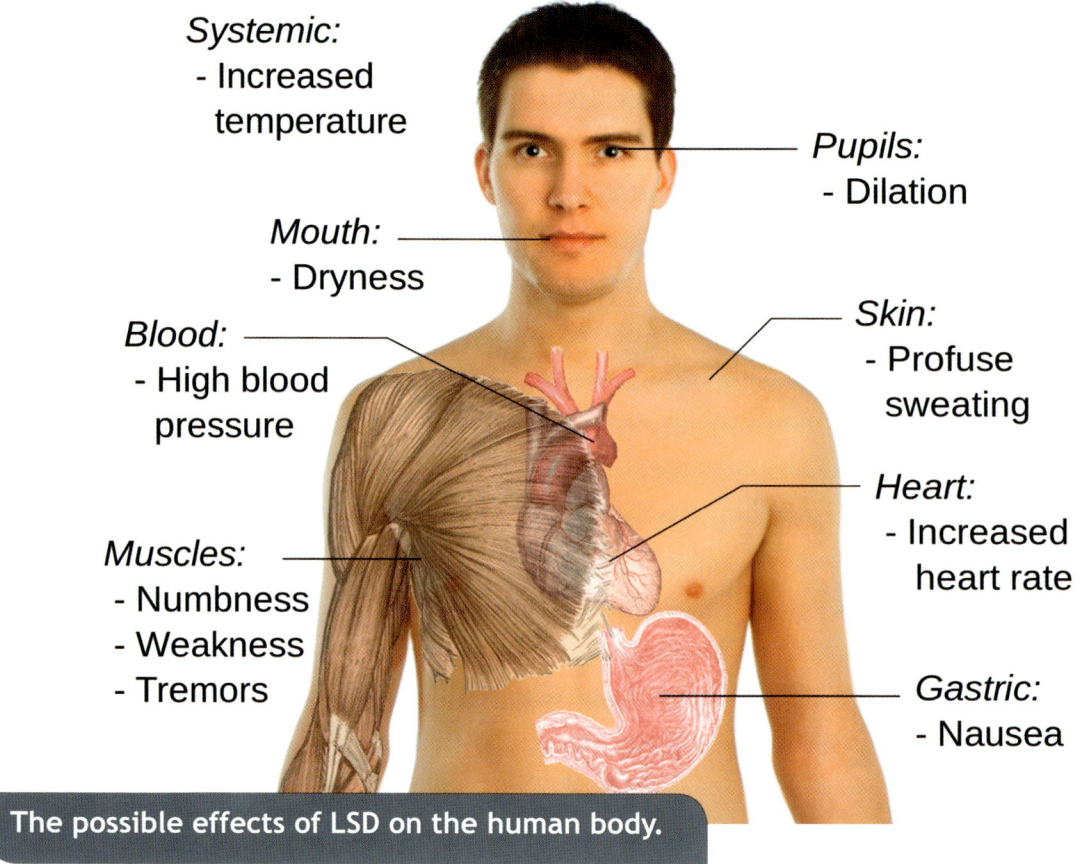

The possible effects of LSD on the human body.

the same effect. Higher doses increase the risk of bad side effects and can quickly become dangerous. Also, users can become psychologically dependent on LSD. A person may associate LSD use with certain people, and may make a habit of using the drug in certain situations. This can make quitting difficult, since it may require that the user avoid "triggers," such as friends who use LSD.

MESCALINE

While LSD is synthetic, other hallucinogens occur naturally. One is a cactus called peyote, which Native Americans and Native Mexicans, including the Wixáritari, often use in religious ceremonies. Each year at the end of the rainy season, the Wixáritari travel to a tiny village in Mexico in the sacred lands of the Wrikuta, where they believe the world began. As they make their pilgrimage, they gather peyote. The plant grows robustly in the deserts of the American Southwest and Mexico. The plant is small and spineless. It grows underground with only its crown visible on the surface.

On top of the cactus are disc-shaped buttons that the Wixáritari cut. They dry the buttons, chew them, or soak them in water to produce a hallucinogenic liquid. The active ingredient in peyote is **mescaline**, and it has been used for thousands of years in religious rituals. On this journey, the faithful will ingest the plant to purify their sins and to communicate with gods and ancestors.

People like to take mescaline because of the "visions" it induces. Many Native American and Native Mexican people have used mescaline for

A flowering peyote cactus.

This photo of Lophophora williamsii, or peyote, shows just how much of the plant is hidden underground.

centuries as a rite of passage. The Plains Indians, for example, use the peyote plant to go on a "vision quest," which is an ancient way for a person to find spiritual guidance and create a deep understanding of one's purpose on Earth.

Those who eat peyote for religious purposes usually ingest no more than 100 milligrams of mescaline. Consuming 10 to 20 grams of dried peyote buttons, or 0.3 to 0.5 grams of mescaline, will cause a person to hallucinate. Like LSD, there is no way to predict accurately what type of side effects might occur.

Those who take mescaline often experience two phases of intoxication. The first is a period in which the person experiences a feeling of well-being and sharpened senses. The next phase is hallucinogenic, in which the person might see colorful objects and shapes. Under the influence of mescaline, users may lose coordination, since their perception of space and time is skewed. People do not lose consciousness after ingesting mescaline, nor will they lose the control of their limbs and senses. Unlike other drugs that can make a person violent, mescaline users typically do not lash out.

Like LSD, peyote is not considered an addictive drug. Addiction is characterized by an inability to stop using a drug. The mind and body both crave the drug's effects and getting the drug becomes central to the user's

CHAPTER TWO: LSD AND OTHER CLASSIC HALLUCINOGENS

life. While mescaline is not addictive with sustained use, it can interfere with regular day-to-day activities. It can also cause poor eating and sleeping habits. Users can also experience a bad trip, which might cause them to act out in an irrational and even unsafe manner.

Like LSD, short-term negative side effects of mescaline use include anxiety, panic, and a loss of sense of one's self and one's environment. Chronic mescaline intoxication can results in symptoms such as loss of motivation, mood disturbances, and flashback hallucinations.

PSILOCYBIN OR MUSHROOMS

As you read in the first chapter, psilocybin is the main ingredient in "magic mushrooms." While ancient societies pioneered the use of mushrooms in their religious ceremonies, many teens and adults continue to search for the mind-altering effects psilocybin produces.

The psychedelic mushroom called *Psilocybe mexicana*.

Psilocybin is an organic compound that occurs naturally in roughly 200 species of mushrooms. The body quickly converts, or **metabolizes**, the compound into psilocin, a type of alkaloid. Psilocin has mind-bending properties, just like LSD and mescaline, that induce euphoria and visual hallucinations.

Scientists once thought that psilocybin caused the brain to ramp up its activity. But in 2012, British researchers found the opposite happens. In a study published in the *Proceedings of the National Academy of Sciences*, researchers said activity drops in certain parts of the brain under the influence of psilocybin. The drug affects the regions of the brain that control our senses. A normally functioning brain limits what a person sees, hears, and feels, the scientists said. It keeps a person's world and experiences in order. Psilocybin cuts these connections, allowing a person's senses to run wild. "The results seem to imply that a lot of brain activity is actually dedicated to keeping the world very stable and ordinary and familiar and unsurprising," said Robin Carhart-Harris, the study's lead author.

BAD "SHROOMS"

It would be hard for a person to overdose on the psilocybin in mushrooms, but it can cause panic attacks and other adverse reactions. One study by researchers in the United Kingdom documented an outbreak of psilocybin ingestion. In the study, 44 patients went to the hospital due to psilocybin ingestion over a five-week period. Forty of the patients had symptoms of extreme eye dilation, and about half of the patients had signs of increased blood pressure and heart rate. Twenty-three of the patients experienced nausea and vomiting. The effects of the mushrooms were short-lived and wore off after 12 hours in all but one of the patients.

Magic mushrooms can be toxic and deadly when consumed in very large doses. The lethal dose of mushrooms is about 1.5 times that of caffeine. On average, a person weighing 160 pounds would have to eat about 37 pounds of magic mushrooms to be at risk of dying.

TEXT-DEPENDENT QUESTIONS

1. Which parasitic fungus did researchers use to synthesize LSD?
2. What is mescaline?
3. According to British researchers, how does psilocybin affect the brain?

RESEARCH PROJECT

Write a biography of either Albert Hofmann or Timothy Leary. What influences did they have on American popular culture?

WORDS TO UNDERSTAND

benign: not a threat to life or long-term health.

empathy: the ability to identify or understand another person's feelings.

methamphetamine: an illegal stimulant.

CHAPTER THREE
ECSTASY (MDMA)

"My name is Michelle C. I am 17 years old and have been in recovery for over a year and a half. I tried many drugs when I was active but the one that I liked the most was Ecstasy." With those words, Michelle gained the attention of a group of U.S. senators. It was March 21, 2001, and a Senate committee was hearing firsthand accounts of those who used Ecstasy, one of the most popular mind-altering drugs in the world. At the time, Ecstasy was becoming very popular among young people.

Michelle told lawmakers her former boyfriend first introduced her to the drug. It made her feel as if she didn't have any problems. "Everything was wonderful," she said. "I had no inhibitions while I was under the influence. What my boyfriend did not tell me was that I would want to take Ecstasy all the time."

Michelle soon felt as if she couldn't live without the drug. She stole money from her parents to buy the pills. She cut classes to get high. "The good feelings I was getting from Ecstasy were making me act out in ways that were damaging to myself and the people that cared about me. Feeling wonderful meant that I had to lie, cheat, and steal."

36 HALLUCINOGENS: ECSTASY, LSD, AND KETAMINE

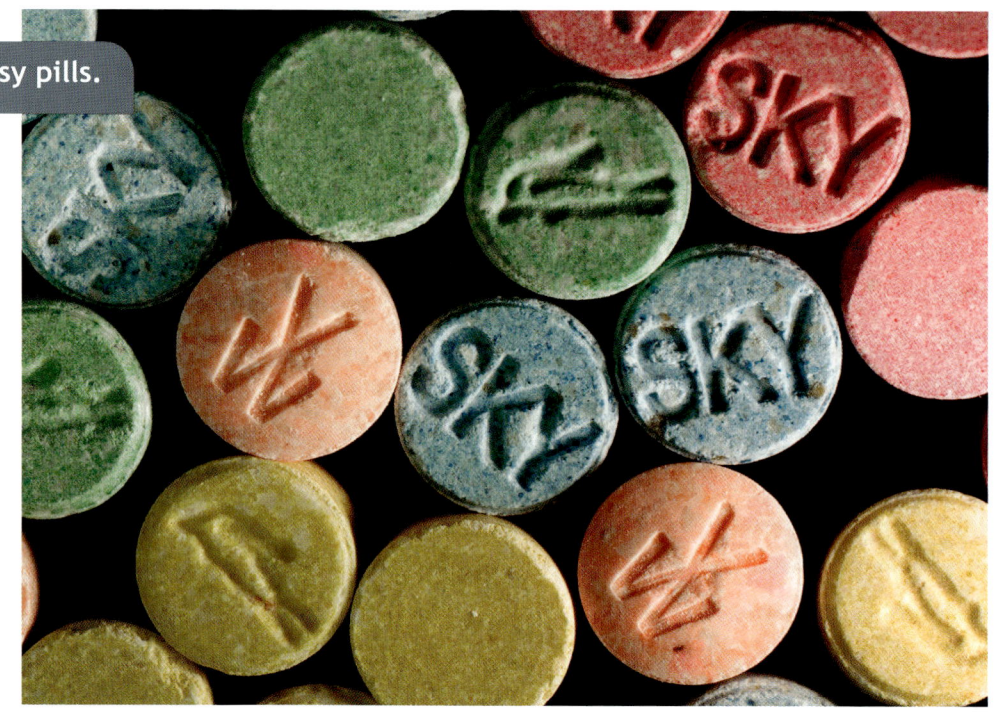

Ecstasy pills.

Ecstasy is a synthetic drug that mimics the effect of stimulants, such as amphetamines, while causing hallucinogenic effects similar to mescaline. Ecstasy goes by many names, including "Molly," "E," "XTC," "X," "hug drug," and "love drug." The main ingredient in Ecstasy is a chemical compound called methylene dioxy methamphetamine, or MDMA. It is a derivative of the synthetic stimulant methamphetamine. Pure MDMA is a pure white powder. Most Ecstasy pills or capsules contain less than 100 milligrams of MDMA, and they come in various forms and colors. Most, if not all, Ecstasy pills and capsules contain other substances and drugs, such as food dye, amphetamine, and caffeine.

A SHORT HISTORY OF MDMA

German scientists at the pharmaceutical company Merck first patented the compound in 1912. Most people think MDMA was manufactured as an appetite suppressant for German soldiers. However, that is a myth. The Germans were looking for a medicine to help blood clot more effectively.

In the 1950s, researchers at the University of Michigan studied MDMA as one of a half-dozen or so chemical compounds that the military thought about using as a possible toxin or stimulant. However, it received little attention, and the military declassified the studies in the early 1970s.

It wasn't until 1976 that a chemist named Alexander Shulgin first developed what we now call Ecstasy while working at Dow Chemical. Shulgin specialized in creating and experimenting with mind-altering drugs, and he had a reputation for trying out his discoveries on himself, his wife, and his friends. He had his first psychedelic experience on mescaline in 1960. He loved how he felt on the drug. "I understood that our entire universe is contained in the mind and the spirit," he wrote later. "We may choose not to find access to it, we may even deny its existence, but it is indeed there inside us, and there are chemicals that can catalyze its availability."

Shulgin discovered a new method for synthesizing Ecstasy in his lab in 1976. He tried it on himself and reported that the drug created an altered state of consciousness. He introduced the drug to Leo Zeff, a psychologist and colleague, hoping it could be used to treat emotional problems such as anxiety. Zeff distributed the drug to therapists across the United States, and they began to use Shulgin's version of MDMA in treating some psychiatric patients. Some psychiatrists called Shulgin's creation "penicillin for the soul," because those who took it were able to gain new insights into their problems. Patients with suppressed memories suddenly remembered them. MDMA created a sense of euphoria, emotional warmth, and empathy. It also distorted space and time.

Word quickly spread about the mind-twisting properties of MDMA, which became widely known as Ecstasy. The fact that Ecstasy was a hybrid drug with both psychedelic and stimulant properties made it especially attractive to those looking to party all night. People started selling their prescriptions of MDMA on the street. Soon drug dealers were making the drug in homemade labs, and they began selling it at all-night dance clubs, parties, "raves," and on the street. By the mid 1980s, Ecstasy use had grown into a major problem. In 1985 the U.S. Drug Enforcement Administration (DEA) banned the drug.

Ecstasy, like LSD, heroin, and cocaine, is viewed by some people as a "culture drug." LSD, for example, was strongly associated with hippies, while heroin was the drug of choice for many punk rockers. Ecstasy is typically associated with the electronic dance movement. In 2014, 1.4 percent of 8th graders said they had tried MDMA, as did 3.7 percent of 10th graders and 5.6 percent of 12th graders.

HOW DOES ECSTASY WORK?

Once a person takes a hit of Ecstasy, it takes about 15 minutes for MDMA to travel to the brain. As it does, the drug increases the activity of three neurotransmitters: dopamine, serotonin, and norepinephrine. Serotonin plays a role in a person's mood, while dopamine is often called the "feel good" neurotransmitter, because it can make you feel wonderful when your body produces it in balanced amounts. Norepinephrine works like adrenaline, which the body releases when a person is excited, fearful, or angry. Norepinephrine narrows the body's blood vessels and increases blood pressure and sugar levels. It gives a person more energy.

MDMA revs up the production of all three of these chemicals, especially serotonin. The increase in serotonin causes a euphoric feeling. As a result, users feel highly sensual. They may want to kiss, hug, and caress others, which is why many people call Ecstasy the "hug drug," or the "love drug."

Many Ecstasy users claim that the drug allows people to emotionally bond with one another. It's a process called *empathogenesis*. Some people use the drug primarily for this feeling. It allows awkward people to deal

CHAPTER THREE: ECSTASY (MDMA) 39

MDMA is strongly associated with DJ and rave culture, where it's sometimes called "Molly."

with others more easily. Like other hallucinogens, it also enhances a person's senses. Those on the drug may run their hands over objects, or continually taste and smell food and drink due to these heightened sensations.

THE RISKS

Some people have bad experiences on Ecstasy. "Ann" told the Foundation for a Drug-Free World that "Ecstasy made me crazy. One day I bit glass, just like I would have bitten an apple. I had to have my mouth full of pieces of glass to realize what was happening to me. Another time, I tore rags with my teeth for an hour." Another user, Frankie, noted that things changed after he used Ecstasy for a few years. "The quality started getting bad and a lot of the pills started feeling really speedy. It was never as good as that first time."

People often believe that Ecstasy is a benign recreational drug. But it isn't. It can make a person do things he or she normally wouldn't do. It can also affect a person's body. One of the most common dangers is the risk of overheating (hyperthermia), which can shut down the kidneys, liver, or heart. Ecstasy interferes with the body's ability to regulate its own temperature, and it also makes it hard to see the warning signs of overheating. Someone high on Ecstasy may not notice that their body is getting hot and sweaty, and they may not try to cool off or drink water. The increase in body temperature can be made much worse from the user's activity, such as dancing in a crowded space, while on the drug.

Ecstasy causes an increase in serotonin levels, which often makes people more affectionate.

HEALTH EFFECTS

This chart from the National Institute on Drug Abuse outlines the possible health effects of taking MDMA.

POSSIBLE HEALTH EFFECTS

Short-term effects	enhanced sensory awareness; confusion; depression; sleep problems; anxiety; increased heart rate and blood pressure; muscle tension; teeth clenching; nausea; blurred vision; faintness; chills or sweating; rise in body temperature leading to liver, kidney, or heart failure and death
Long-term effects	confusion, depression, memory, and sleep loss; increased anxiety, impulsiveness, or aggression; loss of appetite; less interest in sex
Withdrawal Symptoms	fatigue, loss of appetite, depression, trouble concentrating

Source: National Institute on Drug Abuse, "Commonly Abused Drugs Chart." http://www.drugabuse.gov/drugs-abuse/commonly-abused-drugs-charts#mdma.

That's what happened on February 22, 2015, when students at Wesleyan University in Middletown, Connecticut, had to be hospitalized after attending a party and downing large amounts of Ecstasy. Ten Wesleyan students and two others were hospitalized with symptoms of overdose, forcing the university to send an e-mail to students warning about the "complications arising from the use of a version of the drug Molly, a refined and more powerful form of Ecstasy." The next day police arrested four students for distributing the drug.

Some students feared that their classmates might have fallen victim to a tainted version of Ecstasy. Many times, drug dealers will mix MDMA in pills and capsules with other substances, such as rat poison or caffeine. The other chemicals they use can be toxic. Whether the Wesleyan students were right or not, their concerns highlighted another risk of taking Ecstasy: users may not have any idea what they are taking. In 2012, eight people died in Alberta, Canada, after taking a drug they thought was Ecstasy, but that actually contained high doses of a toxic amphetamine called "Death."

The MDMA compound by itself can cause a number of physical and mental side effects, including anxiety, irritability, sadness, aggression, and sleeplessness. It can cause muscles to cramp and teeth to clench. Researchers studying MDMA's effect on animals have concluded that the drug can damage brain cells containing serotonin. Some studies suggest the effects of MDMA on serotonin are long-lasting and can occur in humans as well. However, it is difficult to measure serotonin levels in humans.

Some studies show that people who have used MDMA for long periods can become confused, depressed, or forgetful. These conditions, scientists surmise, occur because the drug ultimately slows the body's production of serotonin.

Whether or not Ecstasy is addictive is often debated. Experts say it has addictive qualities because it targets the same neurotransmitters that other addictive drugs, such as heroin, target. Over the years, researchers

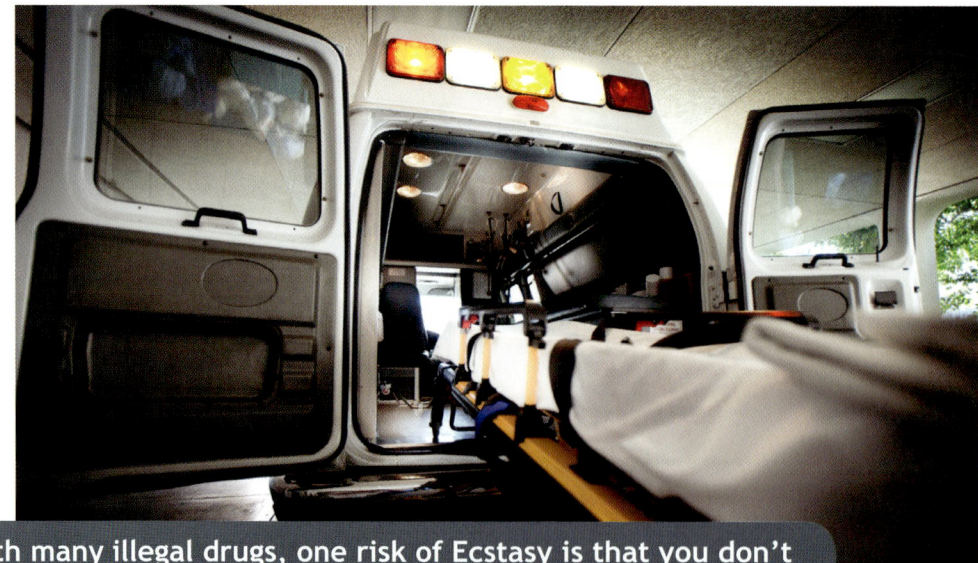

As with many illegal drugs, one risk of Ecstasy is that you don't always know for sure what's actually in the dose you're taking. Dealers sometimes mix in toxic chemicals along with the MDMA.

have attempted to figure out how many people have become physically dependent on Ecstasy, but the studies that have been conducted offer varying results. Still, users can become tolerant to Ecstasy, which means that they need higher and higher doses to get the same effects. And with higher doses comes higher risks.

Ecstasy users may also turn to other drugs, such as heroin or cocaine, to cope with the mental and physical discomfort that results after one "comes down" from Ecstasy. It has been estimated that over 90 percent of Ecstasy users also take other, highly addictive drugs. Like LSD and other psychedelics, Ecstasy can also cause psychological dependence. Ecstasy users may believe that they need it to feel good, which can cause them to keep using it despite experiencing unpleasant effects.

TEXT-DEPENDENT QUESTIONS

1. In what year did scientists first synthesize MDMA?
2. Why is Ecstasy often called the "love drug" or the "hug drug"?
3. Name three possible health effects of using Ecstasy.

RESEARCH PROJECT

Learn more about Ecstasy and create a public awareness campaign about the use of the drug. You might create a poster, a computer presentation, or a video presentation.

WORDS TO UNDERSTAND

anesthetics: a group of drugs that dulls the sensation of pain and might cause unconsciousness.

catatonia: a trance-like state.

grandiose: overly ambitious or extravagant.

hyperactive: unusually active, restless, and lacking the ability to concentrate for any great length of time.

limbic system: the portion of the brain that deals with emotions and memories.

paranoid: unreasonably suspicious of other people.

psychotic: a person who is delusional and whose perception of reality is distorted.

CHAPTER FOUR

DISSOCIATIVE DRUGS

In Stamford, Connecticut, a drug dealer bites a police officer and injures another after they chase him through the woods. In Houston, Texas, a man fleeing from the police drives 15-20 mph only to stop the car abruptly to let a bunch of baby ducklings cross the street. In Oklahoma City, a mother leaves her children inside an unlocked car to run a brief errand, and returns to find the car gone. The car reappears a few minutes later with the children unharmed and a disoriented woman behind the wheel, who was described by local reporters as "not coherent" with a "blank stare on her face."

Police said each of these people were high on PCP, more commonly known as "angel dust." PCP is a dissociative drug. Dissociative drugs distort a person's senses and make it seem as if they are detached from reality. The drugs are more correctly called "dissociative anesthetics." Such drugs do not involve a loss of consciousness, but they do produce a lack of sensation to pain, amnesia (memory loss), and catatonia.

46 HALLUCINOGENS: ECSTASY, LSD, AND KETAMINE

PCP

Scientists developed PCP, whose laboratory name is phencyclidine, in the 1950s as an anesthetic that could be injected directly into a person's veins. However, doctors stopped using PCP in the late 1970s because patients often became delusional, agitated, and irrational. Many went into **psychotic** fits.

Today, PCP has no medical value, but it is a highly risky recreational drug, a white bitter-tasting crystalline powder sold illegally in tablets and capsules. PCP can also be sold in liquid or powder forms. It is easy to dissolve in water. Users can inject or snort PCP, or they "lace" (combine) the drug with tobacco or marijuana. Experts say a low dose of PCP consists of 3-5 milligrams, while 5-10 milligrams is the most common dose. People will usually smoke or inject the lower doses of PCP, while heavier doses are taken orally.

PCP comes in a few different forms including powder and pills. Compare this photo to the one on page 36. Notice how similar they are? The colorful pills that are sold as Ecstasy can sometimes be PCP in disguise.

PSYCHOLOGICAL SIDE EFFECTS OF PCP

According to the University of Maryland's Center for Substance Abuse Research, psychological effects of PCP include the following:
- mild to intense euphoria
- relaxation or drowsiness
- feelings of unreality and dissociation with the environment
- distorted sense of one's body, including a feeling of weightlessness
- distorted sense of time and space
- visual and auditory hallucinations and other sensory distortions
- difficulty concentrating and thinking
- anxiety
- agitation
- paranoid thoughts
- confusion and disorientation
- intense feelings of alienation
- depression
- bizarre or hostile behavior
- obsession with trivial matters
- grandiose delusions
- panic, terror, and an overwhelming fear of imminent death

Source: Center for Substance Abuse Research (CESAR), "Phencyclidine (PCP)." http://www.cesar.umd.edu/cesar/drugs/pcp.asp.

PCP's heyday was back in the late 1970s and the 1980s. During the 1990s, there was a steep drop in the number of people using the drug, but in recent years, those numbers have moved steadily upward. In 2006, 70,000 people aged 12 and older admitted to taking the drug for the first time. That number skyrocketed to 123,000 in 2012, only to decline in 2013 to 32,000, according to the Substance Abuse and Mental Health Services Administration.

PHYSICAL SIDE EFFECTS OF PCP

The Center for Substance Abuse Research also notes the following effects of PCP on the body:
- impaired motor skills
- blurred vision and dizziness
- a painful reaction to sound
- blank staring
- speech disturbances, ranging from difficulty articulating to incoherent speech or inability to speak
- muscular rigidity
- decreased sensitivity to and awareness of pain, touch, and position
- stupor or coma
- irregular heartbeat
- alternately abnormally low and abnormally high blood pressure
- slow, shallow, and irregular breathing
- doses may result in an overdose and lead to coma, convulsions, or death

Source: Center for Substance Abuse Research (CESAR), "Phencyclidine (PCP)." http://www.cesar.umd.edu/cesar/drugs/pcp.asp.

EFFECT ON THE BRAIN

PCP impacts several neurotransmitters, including glutamate, dopamine, norepinephrine, and serotonin. The chemical composition of PCP increases the level of dopamine, norepinephrine, and serotonin by blocking the ability of neurons to "uptake" the chemicals. It also inhibits the action of glutamate by blocking a specific receptor called N-methyl-D-aspartate, or NMDA.

PCP mainly acts by inhibiting the effects of glutamine, which plays an important role in the perception of pain, as well as in learning, memory, and emotion. PCP also creates excess dopamine in the brain, which is believed to be the reason why users experience feelings of euphoria and demonstrate psychotic behaviors. The increase in norepinephrine results in high blood pressure, rapid heart rate, and **hyperactivity**.

PCP users often feel numb, as if they are moving through life in a cloud. They can become catatonic and drooling, or suddenly unpredictable. The drug is long-lasting, and it can take several hours before it wears off.

MYTHS VERSUS REALITY

People have blamed PCP for spurring mindless acts of violence, including cannibalism, decapitations, and eye-gouging. Criminals supposedly high on PCP are said to have terrified police with superhuman strength. Some tales even have describe PCP users ripping off their handcuffs. Many of these stories are often exaggerated.

While PCP does induce psychotic delusions and paranoid behavior, studies show that it increases aggressive and violent behavior in people already prone to aggression and violence. Most PCP users are not violent by nature and become disoriented because of the drug. Moreover, there is no evidence suggesting PCP increases a person's muscle power. In fact, the only study done on the subject concluded that the grip strength of laboratory mice given PCP actually decreased. Scientists agree there are no physiological or physical mechanisms to explain how PCP can affect a person's strength. Since PCP is an anesthetic, it can reduce feelings of pain, but it cannot make a person completely pain free.

ADDICTION AND DEPENDENCY

Unlike other hallucinogens, PCP is addictive. Repeated PCP use may lead to severe cravings and compulsive PCP-seeking behavior such as lying or

50 HALLUCINOGENS: ECSTASY, LSD, AND KETAMINE

stealing. A PCP user might also become isolated from his or her friends. Long periods of misuse will impact a person's memory and speech, and it can contribute to weight loss.

Scientists say it doesn't seem as if PCP creates as severe physical dependency as drugs like heroin do. However, PCP can lead to physical tolerance and withdrawal symptoms. A person who stops using PCP immediately might become depressed, tired, or have a lack of energy.

KETAMINE

Calvin Stevens knew that PCP was a bust as an anesthetic, so he wanted to find a new drug that could replace it. Stevens, a scientist at Parke-

Vials of ketamine.

REDUCING BRAIN DAMAGE

Dr. Karl Jansen, a member of the Royal College of Psychiatrists and a leading expert on ketamine, has proven that the drug has beneficial effects on the brain when given in the right dose by a trained physician. Ketamine can help prevent brain cell death in people whose brains are getting insufficient oxygen. Moreover, evidence suggests that when the drug is quickly given to a stroke victim, it can reduce damage to the brain.

Davis Laboratories, soon came up with an alternative—ketamine. Once it was approved by the U.S. Food and Drug Administration in 1970, doctors began administering ketamine to soldiers injured during the Vietnam War. The drug allowed doctors to operate on patients by significantly reducing pain without paralyzing their breathing. Still, like PCP, those who took ketamine began to feel detached from reality and disconnected from the environment.

Although the drug has a legitimate medical use as an anesthetic by veterinary doctors—Special K, as it is called, has become a popular "club drug." People can snort it or add it to beverages. Its intoxicating effect can last up to an hour, and it is not as potent as PCP. People began using ketamine as a psychedelic drug in the mid 1960s. Those who used it said ketamine put them in a "trance-like" state.

By the 1990s, ketamine was being made in home-made labs or stolen from veterinary hospitals. Use spread quickly around the United States and elsewhere around the world, and it became one of the sought-after party drugs on the rave and club scene. Some partygoers secretly dump the drug in the drinks of unsuspecting people to take advantage of them sexually. That's why ketamine is often called a "date rape" drug.

A CURE FOR DEPRESSION?

Although ketamine is widely known as a recreational hallucinogen, researchers have begun to study the drug as a potential treatment for depression. Scientists are trying to find out whether the drug can relieve depression in those who have been unsuccessful in using conventional antidepressants such as Prozac and Lexapro.

A few small studies of ketamine have been conducted with depressed patients. In some studies, up to 85 percent of patients experienced relief from depression symptoms, and the effects were far more rapid than the effects of conventional antidepressants. In other studies, however, few patients responded. The goal of current research is to understand exactly how ketamine works so that scientists can produce a safer drug that mimics its effects. Scientists have been somewhat successful, but so far the new drugs don't act as quickly as ketamine. Moreover, researchers aren't sure what the side effects of prolonged ketamine use would be on a person suffering from depression. Besides its mind-altering effects, ketamine can raise a person's blood pressure, decrease brain function, and create bladder problems.

THE "K-HOLE"

Chemically, ketamine is similar to PCP, but its effects do not last as long. Like PCP, ketamine inhibits the effects of glutamate by affecting NMDA receptors. It also blocks the uptake of serotonin and dopamine. The drug blocks the neural pathways between the brain's thalamus, which relays sensory information to the cerebral cortex. The thalamus controls a person's senses, memory, ability to learn, reason, and other functions, including problem solving. Ketamine also stimulates the **limbic system**, the

CHAPTER FOUR: DISSOCIATIVE DRUGS

neural structures in the brain that are involved in determining a person's emotional behavior.

Those who use the drug report feeling an out-of-body sensation, as though they are floating above themselves. Such a dissociative reaction is what many people seek. Sometimes, though, these "trips" can go bad and be terrifying. It's a weird feeling that users call the "K-hole."

The journalist David Eggins has been through the K-hole. Writing in *The Guardian*, a London newspaper, Eggins, a Special K user, said "nothing can prepare you for the chaos" of the K-hole. "The K-hole has been described as an endless dimension to explore, and that's exactly what it is," Eggins writes. "Space, time and language either have no meaning or become ridiculously distorted. It can seem as if you are travelling through time or

A gram of ketamine crystals.

seeing into the future, as if you are living multiple lives or not living at all." The problem, Eggins said, is that none of that was real.

ADDICTION

Those who use ketamine regularly can develop signs of tolerance, which means they need more of the drug to produce the same feelings. The drug can also produce a mental or psychological craving. Both tolerance and craving are signs of addiction. In many cases, the psychological addiction created by the drug can often lead to a person continuing to use it, despite experiencing significant consequences.

However, unlike drugs such as heroin, ketamine does not seem to produce prolonged physical withdrawal symptoms once a person stops using the drug. Users have reported bouts of tension, a poor attention span, and restlessness when coming off the drug.

SALVIA

One day, an 18-year-old girl smoked a joint (marijuana) with her boyfriend. Hours later, she was admitted to a psychiatric hospital, agitated, disorganized, and hallucinating. While in the psychiatric hospital, the woman began to self-mutilate, cutting and injuring herself. Doctors gave her large doses of antipsychotic drugs, yet she continued to have delusions, disordered thinking, and slow speech. Nothing seemed to work, including two doses of electroconvulsive treatments, in which doctors administered jolts of electricity to her brain.

The young woman grew increasingly disturbed. She bit off part of her tongue and swallowed it. Her blood pressure dropped and an X-ray showed that she suffered from peritonitis, an inflammation of the abdominal lining. Parts of her abdomen and colon were dying and required surgical removal.

CHAPTER FOUR: DISSOCIATIVE DRUGS

After a long hospitalization, her symptoms decreased and she was released in stable condition. And doctors soon learned the reason for her bizarre behavior. It turns out she wasn't just smoking marijuana the day she was admitted to the hospital. Her boyfriend had slipped a dose of *Salvia divinorum* into her joint. While most people would not go through the physical and mental torture this woman did after ingesting the hallucinogen, it was dangerous for her both because she was young and because she had "dosed" on it. Dosing is the dangerous practice of giving an unsuspecting person a drug. The woman didn't know what was happening to her. Dosing is illegal, and the woman and her family instituted legal proceedings against the boyfriend.

Salvia is an herb that Native Mexicans have used for thousands of years for its entheogenic effects. It can be rolled into cigarettes and smoked. It can also be put into a pipe and inhaled. People can chew its leaves or drink its juice.

The salvia plant's active ingredient, salvinorin A, is as potent as LSD. Unlike LSD, Ecstasy, PCP, and other hallucinogenics, salvia is legal in most

Dried salvia plant.

states, which is why it is gaining popularity with teenagers. In 2014, 0.6 percent of 8th graders admitted using salvia, as did 1.8 percent of 10th and 12th graders.

Salvia's impact on the brain is intense. Salvia users might see bright lights and vivid colors and shapes. They might laugh uncontrollably and hallucinate. The experience is described as psychedelic, with rapid changes in visual perception, mood and body sensations, emotional swings, feelings of detachment, and decreased ability to interact with one's surroundings. Although salvia is generally considered a hallucinogen, it does not act on serotonin receptors that are activated by other hallucinogens, including LSD, and its effects are described as quite different from other hallucinogens.

Researchers at the U.S. Department of Energy's Brookhaven National Laboratory conducted a study in 2008 to see just how salvia affects the brain. Using anesthetized primates, scientists administered a radioactive version of salvinorin A and used a PET scanner to track its neural effects.

Crystals of salvinorin A, which is derived from salvia, viewed under a microscope.

CHAPTER FOUR: DISSOCIATIVE DRUGS   57

In less than a minute, the drug had made its way to the brain. It moved through the body 10 times faster than cocaine. Within 16 minutes, the drug was gone, giving researchers an indication of why people who use the drug report an immediate high that starts to fade away within 10 minutes.

The drug mostly impacted the parts of the brain that control motor function and sight. While other hallucinogens create a euphoric feeling, salvia does not. The drug does target receptor sites in the brain that control pain. And unlike Ecstasy and other party drugs, salvia does not promote a desire to connect with others. Those who use salvia describe it as a very personal and isolating experience.

"Most people don't find this class of drugs very pleasurable," Brookhaven chemist Jacob Hooker said. "So perhaps the main draw or reason for its appeal relates to the rapid onset and short duration of its effects, which are incredibly unique."

TEXT-DEPENDENT QUESTIONS

1. How do people use PCP?
2. How might Ketamine alleviate a person's depression?
3. Why isn't salvia considered a party drug?

RESEARCH PROJECT

Research and write a report comparing how Native Americans and Native Mexicans use *Salvia divinorum*, and the way early American civilizations used "magic mushrooms." Describe how each used the hallucinogenic substances. Explain the differences or any similarities.

FURTHER READING

BOOKS

Barter, James: *Hallucinogens*. San Diego, CA: Lucent, 2002.

Cefrey, Holly. *Hallucinogens and Your Neurons: The Incredibly Disgusting Story*. New York: Rosen Publishing, 2001.

Harmon, Daniel E. *Hallucinogens: The Dangers of Distorted Reality*. New York: Rosen Publishing, 2009.

Lockwood, Brad. *Ketamine: Dangerous Hallucinogen*. New York: Rosen Publishing, 2007.

Monroe, Judy. *LSD, PCP, and Hallucinogen Drug Dangers*. New York: Enslow Publishing, 2000.

Olive, M. Foster. *LSD*. Drugs: The Straight Facts. New York: Chelsea House, 2008.

ONLINE

Drugs.com. "PCP (Phencyclidine)." http://www.drugs.com/illicit/pcp.html.

Ketamine Advocacy Network. http://www.ketamineadvocacynetwork.org/.

KidsHealth. "What You Need to Know about Drugs: Ecstasy." http://kidshealth.org/kid/grow/drugs_alcohol/know_drugs_ecstasy.html.

National Geographic. "Magic Mushroom Medicine." http://channel.nationalgeographic.com/drugs-inc/videos/magic-mushroom-medicine/.

National Institute on Drug Abuse. "DrugFacts: Hallucinogens—LSD, Peyote, Psilocybin, and PCP." https://www.drugabuse.gov/publications/drugfacts/hallucinogens-lsd-peyote-psilocybin-pcp.

EDUCATIONAL VIDEOS

Access these videos with your smartphone or use the URLs below to find them online.

"Psychoactive drugs: Hallucinogens." Khan Academy Medicine. "Learn about ecstasy, LSD, and other hallucinogenic drugs and how they influence the body, brain, and behavior." https://youtu.be/GUwV0gibLx8

"Drugged - High on Ecstasy," National Geographic Channel. "See how deep the rabbit hole goes."
https://youtu.be/k2tt2usMJm4

"Is LSD Really That Dangerous?," D News. "LSD is a psychedelic drug that was popularized in the 1960's. What are the effects, and is it really dangerous?"
https://youtu.be/OIfk6M7k77U

"Hidden Dangers of Party Drug 'Molly'," CNN. "CNN's Drew Griffin investigates the hidden dangers of the popular party drug 'Molly.'"
https://youtu.be/dE1PNgp1v00

"Ketamine," The Drug Classroom. "Ketamine is a dissociative anesthetic that has been widely used in recreational and medicinal settings for decades."
https://youtu.be/oX-Xom4fZIU

SERIES GLOSSARY

abstention: actively choosing to not do something.

acute: something that is intense but lasts a short time.

alienation: a sense of isolation or detachment from a larger group.

alleviate: to lessen or relieve.

binge: doing something to excess.

carcinogenic: something that causes cancer.

chronic: ongoing or recurring.

cognitive: having to do with thought.

compulsion: a desire that is very hard or even impossible to resist.

controlled substance: a drug that is regulated by the government.

coping mechanism: a behavior a person learns or develops in order to manage stress.

craving: a very strong desire for something.

decriminalized: something that is not technically legal but is no longer subject to prosecution.

depressant: a substance that slows particular bodily functions.

detoxify: to remove toxic substances (such as drugs or alcohol) from the body.

ecosystem: a community of living things interacting with their environment.

environment: one's physical, cultural, and social surroundings.

genes: units of inheritance that are passed from parent to child and contain information about specific traits and characteristics.

hallucinate: seeing things that aren't there.

hyperconscious: to be intensely aware of something.

illicit: illegal; forbidden by law or cultural custom.

inhibit: to limit or hold back.

interfamilial: between and among members of a family.

metabolize: the ability of a living organism to chemically change compounds.

neurotransmitter: a chemical substance in the brain.

paraphernalia: the equipment used for producing or ingesting drugs, such as pipes or syringes.

physiological: relating to the way an organism functions.

placebo: a medication that has no physical effect and is used to test whether new drugs actually work.

predisposition: to be more inclined or likely to do something.

prohibition: when something is forbidden by law.

recidivism: a falling back into past behaviors, especially criminal ones.

recreation: something done for fun or enjoyment.

risk factors: behaviors, traits, or influences that make a person vulnerable to something.

sobriety: the state of refraining from alcohol or drugs.

social learning: a way that people learn behaviors by watching other people.

stimulant: a class of drug that speeds up bodily functions.

stressor: any event, thought, experience, or biological or chemical function that causes a person to feel stress.

synthetic: made by people, often to replicate something that occurs in nature.

tolerance: the state of needing more of a particular substance to achieve the same effect.

traffic: to illegally transport people, drugs, or weapons to sell throughout the world.

withdrawal: the physical and psychological effects that occur when a person with a use disorder suddenly stops using substances.

INDEX

A
acetylcholine 14-15
acid *see* LSD
addiction
  Ecstasy and 42-43
  ketamine and 54
  LSD and 27
  PCP (Angel Dust) and 49-50
  peyote and 30-31
aggression *16*, 18, 42
alcohol 27
alkaloids 10, 14, 22, 32
alternate states 13-14
amnesia 45
amphetamines 13, 36, 42
anesthetics 44-45, 49-51
Angel Dust *see* PCP (Angel Dust)
antidepressants 52
anxiety 31, 37, 42
appetite, loss of 27
attention span 54
Aztecs *12*, 13

B
bad trips 18, 22, 24, 31
benign 34, 40
blood pressure, increased 32, 49
body temperature, increased 27
boomers *see* LSD
brain, effects on 42, 48-49, 51
brainwashing 25

C
caffeine 33
Carhart-Harris, Robin 32
Carod-Artal, Franciso Javier 12
catatonia 44-45, 49
catecholamine 14-15
Center for Substance Abuse Research 48
chemical weapons 25
CIA 25
club drugs 51
cocaine 24, 27, 38, 43, 57
cognitive-behavioral therapy (CBT) 18
Cold War 25
coming down 43
confusion 42
consciousness, states of 13
cortex 15, 52
counterculture 20, 23-25
cravings 49-50, 54
crisis management 18
culture drugs 38

D
date rape drugs 51
DEA (Drug Enforcement Agency) *14*, 22, 38
Death *see* amphetamines
dependence 28, 43, 49-50
depression 17-18, 26, 42, 52
derivatives 20, 22-23
devil's herb (psychedelic toloache) 12
disorientation 49
dissociative drugs 13, 44-57
dizziness 27
DJ and rave culture *39*
dopamine 38, 48-49, 52
doses *see* LSD
dosing 55
Dow Chemical 37
drooling 49
Drug Enforcement Agency (DEA) *14*, 22, 38

E
E *see* Ecstasy (MDMA)
Ecstasy (MDMA) 13-14, 34-43, *46*, 55-57
Eggins, David 53-54
electronic dance movement 38, *39*
emotion 37, 49, 53
empathogenesis 38-39
empathy 34, 37
entheogenic 10, 12, 55
ergot alkaloids 22
euphoria 23, 32, 37, 49, 57
eye dilation 32

F
flashback hallucinations 27, 31
flesh of the gods/flesh of the devil *see* magic mushrooms
forgetfulness 42
Foundation for a Drug-Free World 27, 39-40

G
glutamate 48-49, 52
grandiose 44, 47
grip strength 49
Guatemala 11

H
hallucinate 10, 11, 30, 56
hallucinations 27, 31-32
hallucinogenic 10, 13, 36
hallucinogen persisting perception disorder (HPPD) 15, 17
hallucinogens
  defined 10-19
  dissociative drugs 44-57
  Ecstasy (MDMA) 34-43
  LSD, and other classic 20-33
Harvard Medical School 17
Harvey, Matt 26-27
heart rate, increased 27, 32, 49
heroin 18, 27, 38, 42-43, 50, 54

hippies 38
hits *see* LSD
Hofmann, Albert 22-23
honey, psychedelic 12
Hooker, Jacob 57
HPPD (hallucinogen persisting perception disorder) 15, 17
HPPDonline.com 17
hug drug *see* Ecstasy (MDMA)
human sacrifices 12
hyperactivity 44, 49
hyperthermia 40

I
inhibitions 20, 25, 35
inpatient therapy 18
insomnia 27
intoxication 30-31
irritability 42

J
Jansen, Karl 51
Johns Hopkins University 26

K
Kesey, Ken *24*
ketamine 13, *50*, 50-54
ketamine crystals *53*
K-hole 52-54

L
lacing 46
learning 48-49
Leary, Timothy 24-25
lethal doses 33
Lexapro 52
limbic system 44, 52-53
Linkletter, Art 24-25
Lophophora williamsii *30*
love drug *see* Ecstasy (MDMA)
LSD 13-14, 17-18, 20-28, 38, 55-56
LSD-25 23
LSD blotter paper *14*

lysergic acid diethylamide *see* LSD

M
magic mushrooms 11-13, 18, 31-33
mania 26
marijuana 54-55
Mayas 12
MDMA (methylene dioxy methamphetamine) *see* Ecstasy (MDMA)
medical mushrooms 18
memory 37, 45, 48-50
mental effects, of LSD 26-27
Merck 36
Merry Pranksters *24*
mescaline 13, 20, 28-31, 36
Mesoamerica 11-13
metabolize 20, 32
methamphetamine 34, 36
Mexico 29
MK-ULTRA 25
Molly *see* Ecstasy (MDMA)
mood changes 27, 31
motivation 31
muscle cramping 42
mushroom cults 11-12
mushrooms *see* magic mushrooms
mushroom stones 11-13
mystical experiences 13

N
National Institute on Drug Abuse (NIDA) 21, 41
Native Americans 28-30
Native Mexicans 28-30, 55
nausea 27, 32
neural pathways 18, 52
neurons 14
neurotransmitters 10, 14-15, 38, 42, 48-49

nitrogen 14
N-methyl-D-aspartate (NMDA) 48, 52
norepinephrine 38, 48-49
numbness 27, 49
Nuremberg Code 25

O
Olmecs 12
out-of-body sensations 53
outpatient therapy 18
overdoses 24, 32-33, 41-42
overheating 40

P
pain 45, 49, 57
panic attacks 17, 31, 32
paranoid 44, 47, 49
parasitic 20, 22
Parke-Davis Laboratories 50-51
party drugs 51, 57
PCP (Angel Dust) 13, 17, 45-50, *46*, 55
peritonitis 54
PET scanner 56-57
peyote 28-31
phencyclidine *see* PCP (Angel Dust)
physical effects 26-27, 48, 50
pilgrimages 29
Plains Indians 30
post-traumatic stress disorder 18
Proceedings of the National Academy of Sciences 32
proselytizing 20, 25
Prozac 52
Psilocybe mexicana *31*
psilocybin 18, *26*, 31-33
psychedelics 10, 12-13, 18, 51, 56
psychological effects 28, 43, 47
psychotic 18, 44, 46, 49

INDEX 63

psychotropic 10, 18
punk rockers 38

R
rave culture *39*, 51
reality, sense of 13, 15, 21
receptors 15, 57
recreational drugs 40, 46, 52
religious rituals 12-13, 29-30
restlessness 54
rites of passage 30
rye 22

S
sadness 42
salvia 13, 54-57
Salvia divinorum 55
salvinorin A 55-57
SAMHSA (Substance Abuse and Mental Health Services Administration) 14, 47
Sandoz Pharmaceutical Company 22-24
schizophrenia 27
self, sense of 31
senses, enhancement of 39
serotonin 14-15, 38, *40*, 42, 48, 52, 56
shrooms *see* magic mushrooms
Shulgin, Alexander 37
side effects 27, *28*, 31, 42, 47-49
sleeplessness 42
Soviet Union 25
Spanish conquistadors 13
Special K *see* ketamine
speech 50
spies 25
Stevens, Calvin 50-51
stimulants 20, 24, 36

Substance Abuse and Mental Health Services Administration (SAMHSA) 14, 47
sugar cubes *see* LSD
support-group therapy 18, *19*
suppressed memories 37
synesthesia 15
synthesize 20, 22

T
Tabasco, Mexico *12*
tabs *see* LSD
teeth clenching 42
tension 54
teonanácatl see magic mushrooms
thalamus 15, 52
therapy 18
toads, psychedelic 12
tolerance 27-28, 50, 54
toloache, psychedelic (devil's herb) 12
tremors 27
triggers 28
trips 21-22, 53

U
United States 25, 51
University of Maryland's Center for Substance Abuse Research 47
University of Michigan 37
unpredictability 49
uptake 48, 52
U.S. Department of Energy Brookhaven National Laboratory 56-57
U.S. Food and Drug Administration 51

V
veterinary doctors 51
violence 49
vision quest 30

visions 29-30
visual hallucinations 32
vomiting 27, 32

W
weakness 27
weight loss 50
window pane *see* LSD
withdrawal 27, 41, 50, 54
Wixáritari 29
Wrikuta 29

X
X *see* Ecstasy (MDMA)
XTC *see* Ecstasy (MDMA)

Y
yellow submarine *see* LSD

Z
Zeff, Leo 37

ABOUT THE AUTHOR

John Perritano is an award-winning journalist, writer, and editor from Southbury CT., who has written numerous articles and books on a variety of subjects including science, sports, history, and culture for such publishers as Mason Crest, National Geographic, Scholastic and Time/Life. His articles have appeared on Discovery.com, Popular Mechanics.com and other magazines and Web sites. He holds a Master's Degree in American History from Western Connecticut State University.

ABOUT THE ADVISOR

Sara Becker, Ph.D. is a clinical researcher and licensed clinical psychologist specializing in the treatment of adolescents with substance use disorders. She is an Assistant Professor (Research) in the Center for Alcohol and Addictions Studies at the Brown School of Public Health and the Evaluation Director of the New England Addiction Technology Transfer Center. Dr. Becker received her Ph.D. in Clinical Psychology from Duke University and completed her clinical residency at Harvard Medical School's McLean Hospital. She joined the Center for Alcohol and Addictions Studies as a postdoctoral fellow and transitioned to the faculty in 2011. Dr. Becker directs a program of research funded by the National Institute on Drug Abuse that explores novel ways to improve the treatment of adolescents with substance use disorders. She has authored over 30 peer-reviewed publications and book chapters and serves on the Editorial Board of the *Journal of Substance Abuse Treatment*.

PHOTO CREDITS

Photos are for illustrative purposes only; individuals depicted are models.
Cover Photo: iStock.com/FotografiaBasica
Drug Enforcement Agency: 14; 22; 36; 46; 55
iStock.com: 7 PeopleImages; 12 stockcam; 16 sturti; 19 Rich Legg; 29 kinright; 30 lolloj; 39 miappv; 40 fizia; 42 Scott Kochsiek
Wikimedia Commons: 24 Joe Mabel; 26 Matthew W. Johnson; 28 Mikael Häggström; 31 Alan Rockefeller; 50 Psychonaught; 53 Psychonaught; 56 C. Hazlett